W9-BBY-916

This book belongs to

KENZIE

Zen Pig

Volume 1 / Issue 2

The Wonder We Are

written by:
mark brown

illustrated by:
amy lynn larwig

each copy sold gives
1 person clean water
for 1 year

"Zen Pig : Volume 1 / Issue 2 The Wonder We Are". Copyright © 2015 by Mark Brown. All rights reserved.
No part of this book may be used or reproduced in any manner
whatsoever without written permission except in the case of brief quotations embodied
in critical articles and reviews.

Come say "Hi!" to Zen Pig online:
ZenPigBook.com

Don't forget, Zen Pig loves seeing pictures of his new home and new friends -
#ZenPig on Instagram to send them his way!

Dedicated to Amy, who has access to some of my
Zen-less moments, yet still supports me.

Thank you.

Granted the gift
Of the sun's first light,
Zen Pig sits with a tree
Enjoying the sight.

Passers-by stop
Amidst a morning stroll
To curiously ask, "What's Zen Pig up to
On that green, grassy knoll?"

One said to the other,
"I'm not quite sure."
The other looked excited
And said, "Let's find out more."

"Excuse us, Zen Pig.
Please tell us what you see,
Because to us it appears
To be just a regular old tree."

"Ah," Zen Pig said,
A small smile on his face.
"The tree is just the beginning,
There's much more to embrace.

When I look at this tree
I see every drop of rain,
Every ray of sunlight,
Every bird it will sustain.

Within a glass of water,
There lies a cloud in the sky.
Within every piece of toast,
A farmer on which it relies.

Every plant and every being
Are all intertwined.
The well-being of all
We must bear in mind.

The whole of nature
Is more than it appears.
We must look closely
And keep our minds clear,

Then we will see
The wonder we are;
Our great connection
Even with the stars.

No matter what you see,
Take the time to look close
And you'll be marveled and amazed
By what it will show."

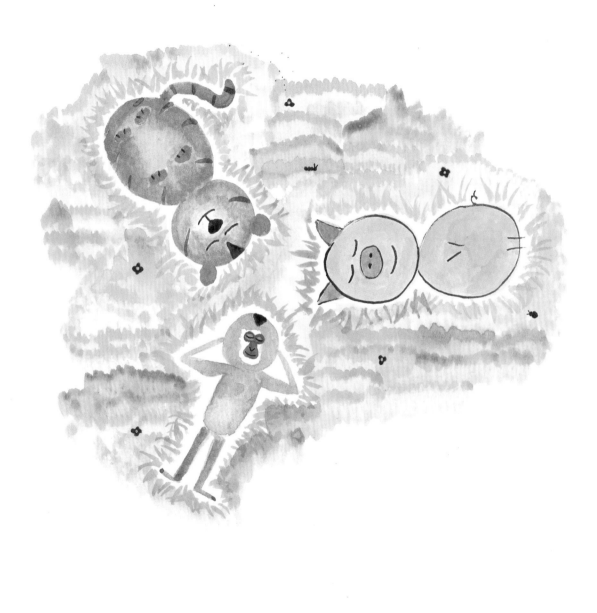

Namaste.

("The light in me loves the light in you.")

_____'s Zen Pig Collection

☐ Zen Pig   ☐ The Wonder We Are   ☐ All That Is Needed

☐ Where You'll Find Love   ☐ Here to Do   ☐ Feelings Are Clouds

It's hard to believe that even today, so many still do not have access to clean water.

But YOU are helping.

Digging new wells, building fences to keep livestock from contaminating sources, repairing existing wells, and constructing toilet slabs give much needed help to communities in need.

Thank You.

What is one thing in nature YOU are grateful for?